# Cassie's COURT

AVELYN PAIGE

CASSIE'S COURT

Avelyn Paige

Copyright © 2016 Lauren Davis as Avelyn Paige

**CREATESPACE EDITION**

Cover Designer: Rebecca Pau of The Final Wrap

Editor and Formatter: Wendi Temporado of Ready, Set, Edit

# dedication

*This book is for those who cancer took too soon. #HopeForACure*

# chapter one

Running down Keady Court, I pass the ball to my shooting guard from the half-court line.

"Good pass, Abby!" yells our coach, just before screaming at Madison, our center. "You're six feet tall, Maddy. Block the damn ball!"

Madison throws her hands up in the air, only to be charged by Becky during a cut to the basket and thrown to the floor, sliding all the way to the baseline on her ass. Coach Beck blows her whistle, sending us all screeching to a halt.

"What the hell do you think you're doing out there, ladies? This isn't a masquerade ball. Stick with who you're guarding and play a little defense. I want to see some actual progress in the backcourt. We have a snowball's chance in hell against Indiana on Saturday if you think what you're doing is playing good D."

1

The ten of us on the floor mutter a collective, "Sorry, Coach," to defuse the situation. "Abby, I want you to trade off with Lauren. I want to try a new play, and I need her speed to make it work."

"Sure thing, Coach," I hesitantly respond. I run toward the bench, giving Lauren a high five as she jogs past me. Settling onto the padded chair, I reach behind my seat and grab a bottle of Gatorade and suck down half the bottle. My heavy breathing finally starts to slow as I watch Coach Beck work with the other girls. Coach constantly yells about not double-teaming key players and leaving key three-point shooters unguarded. We've got our work cut out for us if we want to beat our rivals who have one of the best frontcourts in the Big Ten.

It seems surreal that a small-town girl like me would be playing for a Big Ten school like Purdue. Most of the girls you see on the college courts come from major metropolitan cities, such as Los Angeles and Miami, not from a bustling town of 250 people that the state of Indiana calls the city of Fowlerton. I didn't have the opportunities to play on travel teams or private leagues like some of the girls I play alongside of now, but I have one thing that most pro players lack, Sheer will and determination to play the best I can for my team. It was not until this year—my junior year—that I was given more playing time on the court than warming the bench.

I knew that this year would be my chance to be in the spot light so, I spent most of last summer working myself to exhaustion. My brother and his friends helped me with my shooting drills, along with my defensive plays. It was not until I came back to West Lafayette that I realized how much I'd grown in my skills. It only took three scrimmages before Coach Beck informed me that I was slated to be one of the starters for the team this year.

"I need you to be a leader on and off the court, Abby. Do you think you can handle that?" I recall her asking me the day she sat me down in her office.

From that moment on, I worked my ass off to be the best small forward I could be for my Lady Boilers. After two rough seasons, we worked through the transition of Coach Beck's team agenda and failed recruiting years, and we were finally showing signs of life. We had a good start to our season with an 11-0 preseason record, and are currently sitting at sixth place in the conference with our new record of 21-8, with just one game left in the season to play.

"Let's run it again, ladies. This time, let's try it at full speed, and with fewer screw-ups," Coach Beck yells out at the girls on the court. She observes each player's movements for a little longer before declaring practice over. I stand up and stretch my sore muscles before grabbing my bag to head off to the locker room to shower.

It doesn't take long for me to strip off my sweat-soaked T-shirt and gym socks, which happen to be glued to my body, and head into a shower stall. The hot spray of the water stings as it hits my skin, but after a few moments, my muscles begin to relax. Grabbing my vanilla-scented body wash, I create a bubbly lather between my hands and slowly wash my aching body, taking special care to wash over the growing bruise on my left breast. After the shove into a camera at our game last Saturday, the bruise has yet to heal. Our team doctor had me do a few chest x-rays and an MRI earlier in the week to check for cracked ribs or torn muscles in my chest. I guess, for once, not being top heavy plays in my favor. My boobs may not be the size that of a Playboy model's chest that the guys all lust over, but when one is this bruised and sore, it is a hell of a lot easier to wear a padded sports bra than one with an underwire.

After rinsing off the soap and washing my hair, I step out of the shower and wrap the towel around my body before squeezing the excess water from my long, brown hair. Weaving my way through my teammates, I grab my makeup kit and head to the vanity. I notice that Dr. McGee, our team physician, is in what looks to be a serious discussion with Coach Beck when I walk by her office. Dr. McGee has a stack of papers, along with what looks like x-ray films, scattered around the coach's desk. They stop their conversation and look at me as I pass, which leaves me with an eerie feeling. Did I just see something I wasn't meant to see? Is something wrong with one of my teammates? Both women continue to stare in my direction before Coach Beck rises from behind her desk and closes the blinds.

Shaking off my unease, I finish the short walk to the vanity area and begin to comb out my hair. Deciding on a simple braid, I finish up my beauty routine and head back to my locker to get dressed. Indiana winters are brutal in February, and after the eight inches of snow that fell last night, I know I need to bundle up. Grabbing my fleece-lined leggings, I slip each foot into the legs and pull them up to my waist before grabbing a thicker pair of team sweats and layering them on top. I do the same layering routine with my thermal shirt and hoodie. Bending down to grab my boots, I hear someone clear their throat behind me. I turn to see Coach Beck's worried face.

"I need you to report to my office before you leave, Abby," she murmurs softly.

"Sure, Coach," I reply. "Let me put my socks and shoes on, and I'm all yours. Everything okay?"

Coach's expression doesn't give anything away before she turns to walk back to her office.

*Shit, this is not good. What the hell is going on?*

"What was that about?" my teammate and roommate Lauren asks. "Coach was acting hella weird just now."

"Yeah, Abby. What did you do? Fail a class or something?" Maddy teases while slipping her shirt over her head.

"Maddy, I have no idea what's going on, and unlike you, I have a near perfect GPA of 3.75, baby. What's yours, a 2.5?" I tease back.

Maddy throws her wet towel at me and barely misses me.

"I smell you enough on the court, Maddy. I don't need your stench permanently embedded in my face," I retort. I pick up her discarded towel and toss it back at her.

Maddy snatches the towel in midair and tosses it inside her messy locker. "I don't smell," she counters. "Just because I work this beautiful ass off on the court

5

doesn't mean I reek. Hell, I probably smell like roses after a hard workout."

The room erupts into laughter as she prances around, dancing like a drunken sorority girl during rush week.

"Yeah, *dead* roses," someone yells from the back corner of the locker room. Maddy throws her hands to her hips, feigning offense. "That's not funny! Who said that?" she demands before stomping off to the back of the room.

"Someone call the diva police. Maddy is on rampage again," Lauren whispers. We smile as Maddy questions everyone, looking for the culprit.

Lauren grabs her stuff and starts to head out of the locker room. "Are you in for a movie night tonight, or do you want to go to the Cactus?"

"Movie night. The townies will be out tonight. Plus, the Levee is going to be busy with alumni weekend too. Movies and a Hawaiian pizza sound better than drunken old farts pawing all over me."

"Yeah, good call. Your stalker, Matthew, won't be out anyways. Adam said the frat has a brotherhood ritual or some shit going on tonight. How about I order Mad Mushroom on the way home? Do you want any cheese sticks while I'm at it?" Lauren asks.

"You know, just because the guys can't go out doesn't mean we have to stay in and knit sweaters like spinsters. And yes on the cheese sticks. If we're going to eat our weight in calories, we might as well go big."

"Matthew would take you out if you would just let him. I swear, you bolt every time he mentions the idea of the two of you doing something together, alone," Lauren remarks while rummaging in her purse for her cell phone.

"Matthew's cute, but I don't have time for a relationship. I need to focus on school and playing ball," I respond as I dial her number on my phone. Lauren has this unique ability to lose her phone wherever she goes, especially in her own purse. It's like a deep black hole where everything disappears. I don't know how many times I have threatened to put a bug on her phone, like they do in spy movies, to track it down for her.

Her purse vibrates, and I watch as she digs into its deep, dark depths to get it.

"You have time for a relationship, and you know it. You just don't want to admit that Matthew sets those frilly granny panties of yours on fire. Besides, a guy like that doesn't stay on the market long, so you need to make your move before one of those prissy sorority hoes sinks her teeth into him."

I glare at her and she puts her hands up in defeat.

"All right, I've said my peace on the matter, so I'll see you at home. Text me after your meeting with Coach B."

"I will, and be careful. Becky mentioned the ice polishers were out in full force. We wouldn't want your graceful self to bruise your ass out there. Or your ego."

Lauren flips me the finger as she leaves, causing me to laugh. I notice Coach watching our banter from her office, and deep down, I know making her wait is a bad idea. Coach waits for no one, and that was evident when she left Gabby, our redshirt freshman shooting guard, behind when she was two minutes late for the bus a few weeks ago. Even if you are five minutes early, you are still considered late.

She waves at me to hurry me along, so I gather my backpack and walk to her office. With each step, I internally ask myself what in the hell she could want that would warrant a private meeting. Does Dr. M have something to do with it? Is something wrong with me? Sure, I've had my aches and pains here and there after practice, but I doubt there's anything seriously wrong with me, other than a bruised tit and a flat ass.

I hesitate before I open the door, taking a long, deep breath before knocking.

"Come in."

I slowly open the door.

"You wanted to see me, Coach?" I ask as I quietly close the door behind me.

"Yes. Please, sit down, Abby." She motions to the chair in front of her.

Taking my seat, I toss my backpack onto the floor beside my chair and wait. Coach B sits in silence, like she's thinking something over. She's not the silent type, and I've never known her to be at a loss for words, so I know something is definitely wrong.

Her hands comb through her dark, curly hair before she finally speaks.

"I don't know how to say this, Abby, but Dr. McGee brought me your test results from your scans, and she found something."

Worry sinks deep into the pit of my stomach. "Okay. What is it?"

Her eyes fall to the hardwood desk as she scoots the papers and films toward me.

"What Dr. McGee found is outside our scope of care. She thinks you need to seek the opinion of a specialist."

"An opinion on what, Coach? My bruise? Why would I need to see a specialist over something as trivial as a bruise?" I ask. "It'll just go away with time, won't it?"

"Abby, it's not the bruise Dr. McGee is worried about," Coach whispers. "It's the large mass she found growing inside your left breast."

Her words instantly send shock waves to my brain. A mass? I have a mass in my breast at twenty-one years old. This has to be a mistake. There's no way this should even be happening. It's just a bruise from an on-court injury.

"I know this is a shock to you, but Dr. McGee has set you up with an oncologist first thing in the morning. There's an appointment card with the information in front of you, and I really think you need to go see what they have to say."

Quickly grabbing the stack of papers in front of me, I reach down for my backpack and stuff them inside. I don't even want to look at what they say, because I know as soon as I do, the reality of how bad this could be will set in. I can't bring myself to say the word that came to mind when she said mass. There is no way it could possibly be that.

I stand and quickly rush out of her office as she calls my name, pleading for me to come back. I can't look back and see the pity on her face. I just need to get home. I want to go to sleep so this can all be a bad dream. I'll wake up tomorrow, and this day will only be a nightmare. There's no way in hell my bruise could be that bad. Sure, I took a pretty hard tumble during the game, but how could a bruise go from broken blood vessels to something more serious. They have to be wrong. It can't be cancer.

God, I hope they are wrong.

# Chapter Two

Ten days after meeting with the oncologist Dr. McGee set me up with, I get the call that I need to meet with Dr. Bragg in her office. After a week of non-stop blood draws, tests, and a biopsy, I haven't slept more than a few hours a night. I've been dreading this call since the moment I walked into her cold, drab office.

My mother has been in town since the night I talked to Coach Beck. I called her, bawling my eyes out, as I tried to explain what was going on. She had tried to reason with me, saying that it could be benign, or even a pocket of blood from my bruise, but I couldn't shake the thought that it was something much worse.

Pulling out my phone, I send a quick text to Lauren, and another to my mom.

*Me: Dr. Bragg called. Meeting her at 4.*

*Mom: I'll come pick you up from class. I want to go with you.*

*Me: Mom, it's fine. I'm a big girl. I can take myself to the doctor.*

*Mom: You listen here, young lady. I am coming along, and that's final. Deal with it.*

*Me: Whatever you say, Mom. I'll meet you at Mackey Arena at 3:15.*

Locking my phone, I shove it into the pocket of my hoodie as I walk into my medieval history class. The hour passes quickly, and before I know it, the professor dismisses us. I look down at my notebook to see that I hadn't written a single word on the page. Shit. I spaced out during the entire class. I'll have to ask Maddy for a copy of her notes after practice tonight.

Coach Beck immediately sidelined me after our talk in her office, pending my test results. It pisses me off that she's treating me like a China doll. I need to be on the court, just for a little while, to get my mind off everything. My pleas to her have been ignored, and I nearly lost my mind watching my team almost lose to our biggest rival, IU, last weekend. We got lucky that their star center fouled out. If we would have lost that game, we could have lost our bid to the NCAA tournament. I should have been out there on the floor with my team, not sitting on the bench watching helplessly.

Stowing away my anger over my coach's bullshit decision, I gather my bag and exit the Electrical Engineering Building, and head north toward Mackey Arena. After crossing Stadium Avenue, I see my mom waiting for me at the bus stop area in front of the arena, along with Coach Beck and the entire team. Lauren and Maddy are holding signs covered in glitter with the words, "Abby's Angels."

God, is it too late to turn around and hail a cab? I didn't want a circus to show up and see me off to my appointment, yet here they are, my own personal version of Barnum and Bailey's. It's not that I don't appreciate their support—I understand their need to form a protective and supportive circle around a teammate and friend—I'm just not ready to admit that the big 'C' word may become the new normal for me in less than an hour.

As I walk closer to the crowd, they cheer and clap. I try to plaster on a fake smile to appease them, but I don't have anything to smile about, at least until I talk with Dr. Bragg, who I hope has good news for me.

I stand in silence as my coach and teammates hug me, one by one, before Mom ushers me into the car. We wouldn't want to be late for my date with the devil. Lauren sticks her hand through the open window and grabs my hand.

"No matter what happens," she says, "you and I are in this together." I mutter a quiet thank you as she releases me. Mom starts the car and begins to pull away into the Northwestern Avenue traffic.

The silence in the car is deafening, and I quickly flick on the radio to the local country station. I'm scared, but no one else needs to know how fucking terrified I am. This news could be life-altering.

Twenty minutes later, we pull into the IU Health parking lot. Once we're parked, I try to slide out of the car before Mom can speak, but she grabs me and pulls back.

"I know you're scared, baby, just like I know you're trying to internalize everything like your daddy used to do, but this isn't your mama's first rodeo. I saw that look a thousand times on your dad's face, especially when he knew he would be working in a dangerous part of town. He wanted to spare the rest of us from his worry and pain, just like you're doing right now. You may not want to let me or anyone else in, but if the news is bad, you're going to need us all. You'll need everyone's support to keep your spirits up and help you fight. Baby girl, your brother and I love you very much, and we'll be here every step of the way. All you need to do is let us in."

Tears begin to stream down my face like a cascading waterfall. The thought of losing Daddy to a drunk driver is still devastating. What's worse is that I am the reason we lost him, and the guilt of my actions eat away at me every single day. If I hadn't have rushed out of the house without my gym bag because my brother, Tyler, made me late that morning for my big game, he would still be here now. I called and begged Dad to bring my bag so I could have my lucky pair of socks for the championship game, knowing he would have to rush to make it to work on time. Like always, Daddy never let me down, and his devotion to me is what killed him in the end. He'd still be here if it wasn't for me and my stupid superstitious need to have those goddamn socks that I later burned in anger.

I played my heart out that night because fourteen college scouts were sitting in the stands, and I knew I wouldn't have to burden my financially struggling family with college tuition bills if I played my best. I fought, scrapped, and left everything I had inside of me on that court just to prove to the scouts that I was worthy of their attention and funds. When the buzzer sounded and cemented our win, I was ecstatic and floating on cloud nine. It was the best moment of my life, but it also marked the day my family would never be whole again.

The looks my mom and my brother wore on their faces as they came down to the court to watch me cut down the net at Conseco Fieldhouse told me that something was wrong. I'll never forget that night—being on top of the world, to nose-diving into a pit of rocks. Since that night, I write his badge number on my headband with a Sharpie. 792 will always be my lucky number.

Mom pats my hand and brings me back to reality.

"It's time, baby."

Nodding in agreement, I slide off the leather seat and close the door behind me, but I only take a few steps before I rush into my mother's arms. I hold her body as tight as I can, relishing in the calm she always seems to bring.

"I love you, Mama," I murmur against her chest.

"I love you, baby girl," she whispers against my forehead. Our embrace slowly breaks, and we walk hand in hand into the hospital. We step into the open elevator and hit the button for the oncology floor. As the elevator climbs upward, each ding of a passing floor sends my heart racing.

*It's now or never, Abby. Be the strong girl Daddy raised you to be. If it's bad news, you take the punches and you fight like hell.*

The final ding of the elevator echoes off the metal walls as the doors creep open. We slowly make our way toward the door of Dr. Bragg's office, and I hesitate.

"Is it too late to turn back?" I ask Mom.

She sighs and holds my hand tighter. "No, baby girl, but we need to know, and we aren't going to get answers by waiting around. We'll get through it, whatever the outcome, together."

Without another word, we walk into the bright-blue office and check in with the nurse. What can only be seconds later, a perky nurse calls my name and ushers us back into Dr. Bragg's office.

"Take a seat, Abby. Dr. Bragg will be here in a few moments. She was finishing up with another patient as I left to bring you back. Can I get either of you anything? A bottle of water, perhaps?" the nurse asks politely.

We both decline, and she exits the room. Mom and I sit in complete silence. Every time a set of footsteps approach the office door, I stop breathing. *What if this is it for me? What if it is an untreatable form of cancer? What will I even do with my life? How long would I have to live if it is terminal?* The questions are never-ending with each passing moment, and are only quieted when footsteps fall silent outside the door.

Shit—she's here.

Dr. Bragg breezes into the room and slides into the chair behind her desk. Her weathered face and tired eyes show just how hard her work truly is. She couldn't be much older than my mom, according to the credentials plastered to the walls of her office, but she looks like she could be my grandmother. I doubt delivering potentially life-threatening news, such as a cancer diagnosis, can be easy on a person, or their bodies.

I look over to my mother as she silently prays for good news. Her lips move with such subtlety that I can't read them. Dr. Bragg sees it and waits for her to finish before speaking.

"The Mayo Clinic sent us back your test results this morning. I won't beat around the bush with you, Abby. You strike me as the kind of girl who would rather rip the Band-Aid off instead of slowly peeling it away. I don't have good news for you and your family."

The entire room is shrouded in deafening silence as I wait for her to say the word I've dreaded hearing for over a week now.

"The mass in your breast is malignant. You have Stage 2 breast cancer."

The air feels as if it is being sucked out of my lungs. As if in slow motion, I turn to my mother as she begins to sob into her hands. I simply sit frozen.

"I know it's a shock, especially for someone as young as twenty-one, but your genetic makeup increases your risk for breast cancer. You are positive for both BRCA1 and BRCA2 abnormalities. Even without a family medical history of breast cancer, it is still possible for the genes to be passed down from your mother."

Dr. Bragg looks to my sobbing mother, her face remaining unmarked by emotion.

"Betty, with that in mind, I would recommend that you be tested also. If you are positive, you will need to be under the care of an oncologist to monitor you more closely."

"I don't understand, Dr. Bragg," I whisper. "Are you saying that I developed breast cancer because of my genes?"

Dr. Bragg reaches inside her desk and pulls out a pamphlet and slides it over to me. I pick up the folded paper and hand it directly to my mom.

"In a matter of speaking, yes. Women who have just one of the BRCA gene abnormalities have up to an eighty percent chance of developing breast cancer in their lifetime compared to a twelve percent risk of a woman without the abnormalities. While in the case of your mother, and likely other women in your family, they may have one or both genes, but will never develop breast cancer. It depends on the individual's health, among other factors."

So many questions swarm my mind that I don't know what to ask. Mom folds the pamphlet neatly on her lap as her tears streak down her face and onto the laminated paper.

"Dr. Bragg?" my mom asks.

"Yes, Betty?"

"It says in the pamphlet that women who exercise, eat balanced diets, and avoid alcohol and smoking help lower the risks of breast cancer, even with the bad genes. Abby has played sports her entire life, and has always been a healthy girl. I just don't understand why she has cancer if she's done everything she was supposed to do to not develop it."

Dr. Bragg sighs and quietly contemplates the question. "Cancer is unpredictable. We don't know who will or won't develop it during their lifetimes. Every single type of cancer starts with a genetic mutation, and every person on Earth has six billion cells of various kinds in their body. It takes just one cell mutating and growing exponentially into more cancer cells with each life cycle to create a tumor or a mass."

"So what do we do from here? What are my options?" I ask sheepishly. It's possibly the hardest question I've ever had to ask in my life. It's like walking on a double-edged sword, hoping not to draw blood. I need to know what I am going to be facing, but I would rather go home and hide under my covers than hear the gory details.

"In most cases, I would suggest a surgical procedure called a lumpectomy to remove the mass from your breast, followed by two to three cycles of chemotherapy. But, with having both abnormal genes and the higher risk of recurrence with this kind of cancer, in your case, I would recommend we do a double mastectomy to remove all of your breast tissue."

I gasp. "You want to cut off my boobs? Both of them? Only one has a tumor!"

Dr. Bragg raises her hands in a defensive gesture. "As I said, I know it's an extreme measure, but given your genetics and your age of onset, I think you'd be in the highest percentile for breast cancer to recur after remission. You'd be taking a far greater risk of developing a more advanced breast cancer as well, with the risk of it spreading to other organs, if you decide against the procedure. It is important to note that with technology and your young age, you would be a perfect candidate for reconstructive surgery, should you choose to do so.'"

"How soon do I have to decide? Do I have at least a couple of days to think about it?"

"I'd advise you make the decision regarding the surgery sooner, rather than later. It took until you suffered an injury for symptoms to arise. I know this is all a shock, and a lot to take in, but my advice to you would be to decide within the next few days. Should you decide to move forward with surgery, we could get you scheduled as early as two to three days from now. The choice is ultimately yours, Abby, but I feel that the mastectomy and a short round of chemo will be your best bet for remission and to get you back on the court."

Leaning back into the uncomfortable office chair, I close my eyes and tip back my head. I need a minute to myself in my own mind to mull over the information that has been dumped on me. Do I want to live and go back to playing ball? Of course I do, but knowing massive surgery and chemotherapy is in the cards for me is a daunting reality to grasp. Like Dr. Bragg said, the decision is ultimately mine, and in this moment of pain and panic, I make the single most difficult decision of my life.

Opening my eyes, I look at the two women in the room, both waiting for me to come back to reality and say the words out loud. It's nerve-racking, to say the least. It feels like I am standing in a room full of important people, buck ass naked, completely vulnerable and exposed. I study my mother's pale, grief-stricken face, and I know I can't leave her and my brother alone, especially since Daddy's gone. I am my father's daughter, and I am a fighter to the very end, just like he was.

"Dr. Bragg, please schedule the surgery."

# Chapter three

## Six Weeks Later

"Well, Abby, it looks like you've officially healed from your mastectomy and reconstructive surgery," Dr. Bragg says as she checks my incision sites for what feels like the fifteenth time. Sliding back on her stool, she pulls her purple latex gloves off one by one, and deposits them into the metal trash can behind her while I gently pull on my soft bra and hoodie, attempting to avoid hitting the central line protruding from my chest. If you even so much as brush against it, you get a shockwave of pain from chest to toes. I know it's new, and I'm not used to it yet, but damn, it hurts.

Before Dr. Bragg can turn around, my mom bombards her with questions.

"So, where do we go from here, Doctor? What's her treatment plan going forward?"

I have to admit that as reluctant as I was to have Mom here with me during all of this, she has been my saving grace. After four days in the hospital, recovering from my surgery, she went from caring mother to doting nurse once I was sent home to finish my recovery. Well, my new home. My apartment had a three-story walk-up, so she insisted that she rent a first floor apartment near campus so I could recover more comfortably with all the appointments I had post-op. I fought at first, but after three days at the new place she had rented on a short-term lease, I was grateful for her forward thinking. Climbing those stairs at my apartment would have definitely sucked pain wise, and would have likely lengthened my recovery time. Mom even went to my classes to take notes for me in my absence when my teammates and friends weren't able to do it. Who even does that? I get her taking care of me, but taking my classes as well? It just blows my mind every time I think about it.

"As you know, the additional samples that were analyzed from her mastectomy indicated the cancer was localized to her left breast, as we originally thought. The post-op MRIs show no indication of any additional tumors or areas of inflammation. However, just to be on the safe side, I would suggest the three more rounds of chemo to make sure all our bases are covered."

"Do I really have to do chemo again, Dr. Bragg?" I question, hopeful she might change her mind.

"I'm afraid so. I would rather put you through chemo now than take a chance on any cancer cells that may be lying dormant in other tissues to later resurface as tumors."

Sighing loudly, my mother reaches over and grabs my hand. "I know you don't want to go through that again, baby, but if Dr. Bragg says you need to do it a few more times, then I am in agreement with her."

"I know, Mom. Believe me, I know. I hate the way it makes me feel. I can still smell the puke from when I redecorated the floor mats of your new car after the first round."

"I would much rather you puke on every inch of my car than still have cancer, Abby. You have to remember, that as sick as it makes you, it's helping you beat this bastard of a disease, and it will help you get back to playing basketball. The season may have just ended, but you know you're dying to walk back onto that hardwood floor with your basketball in hand."

Just envisioning being on Keady Court with eighteen thousand fans cheering for my team causes tears to stream down my face. Will I ever be able to play again? Deep down, I know I will, but I still have to consider that cancer may continue to control my life, even with it being surgically removed. My mom pats my hand and brings me out of the dark thoughts running through my mind.

"You'll be back on the court in no time. You just have to keep going with the chemo," Dr. Bragg informs me. "I don't often say this to my patients, but I am fairly positive that long-lasting remission is in your near future."

Easing myself off the exam table, Dr. Bragg's nurse, Kiley, walks me and Mom out the door and directly to the chemotherapy center. Before we walk into the room, my stomach begins to roll. God, I fucking hate this place, and I've only been here once.

*You have to be strong, Abby. Just breathe and be strong.*

Kiley escorts us over to a row of white recliners lined up against a big bay window overlooking the area surrounding the hospital. As comfortable as the chairs may look, they are far from the fluffy La-Z-Boys back at the apartment. They feel more like lightly padded torture chairs after the first hour of sitting in them.

I slide into the chair and settle in as my mom pulls the lever to raise the legs. Mom leans over into my gym bag, that has now been converted into my traveling chemo bag of fun, as I have dubbed it, and pulls out my Purdue fleece blanket, wrapping it around my body in preparation of the chills. I was so cold during my last chemo treatment that I shook the entire time. Mom couldn't take watching me shiver anymore and rushed back home to get my blanket off the couch. Ever since then, my traveling security blanket of warmth has been packed in my bag for every single doctor's appointment.

Nurse Monroe steps up to the side of the chair and cleans the area around my port. With each swipe of the alcohol swab, I wince.

25

"I'm sorry, darlin'," she says with her thick Southern accent. "I know it sucks, but I can't have you getting an infection on top of everything else. I'll tell you that your blood work from your first round came back better than we had anticipated, or Dr. Bragg wouldn't have let you come in today for treatment after your appointment."

"Lucky me," I say, rolling my eyes. "What kind of poison do I get today, Monroe? Is there any way I could persuade you to put saline into my line instead?"

She shakes her head and giggles. "No can do, darlin'. You need to get this medicine into your system, and no matter how much you wanna stall, I ain't switching it to something else. Dr. Bragg's orders."

"Come on, Monroe. It has to be in your nurse's oath that you are supposed to make your patient's feel better, and do you know what would make me feel better? Not taking that shit," I say, pointing to the vial in her hands. Monroe ignores me and draws blood from my port, just as she did before my last treatment.

"Oh, Abby, you think you're so funny. Now be a good girl, and let me get this started so we can get you home. This old broad has a hot date tonight, and I'm not going to miss it because you want to be ornery today," she says. She places a label on the vials and puts the tubes containing my blood into the plastic rack.

"Hot date, huh?"

"Yes, darlin', a hot date. Now, sit back and relax. It's time to let the medicine work its magic." She hooks my central line port to the plastic tubing of the IV bag, then picks up her vial containing the medicine from hell, pulling the entire volume into the syringe, and pushing it into the other line of my port.

"There we go," she coos, putting the syringe on the tray next to her. "Dr. Bragg requested a stronger anti-nausea medicine in your IV today to help with the vomiting. I'll also be sending home a syringe of the same medicine that you can inject into your belly if you start to feel sick again tonight."

"Oh joy, more shots," I groan sarcastically.

"You keep that sassy spirit going, Abby, and you'll be free of me in no time."

Nurse Monroe turns quickly on her heels and heads back toward the nurses' station in the far corner of the room. I think I might have liked her more if I had met her anywhere but here.

Without even saying a word, Mom pulls my iPad from my bag and hands it over to me. The next six hours are going to be torture, but at least I have an endless supply of shows to watch on Amazon Prime, along with a ton of books. I guess that would be the most positive thing to come out of this whole mess; I've finally started reading again. After college started, I had to give up one of my hobbies to dedicate more time to my classes and basketball practice. Nowadays, the only thing I have the time to read is a playbook or a textbook, and we all know how mentally stimulating those two things can be.

Looking around the room, I see so many people with hopeless looks on their faces. The age range is wide for today's treatment. I watch as a young woman sobs quietly while watching her small son scream at the top of his lungs from the needle being placed in his arm. I can see her desperation, wanting so bad to hold and comfort her little boy. It's heartbreaking to be in this room for hours, watching people being brought in and out, with the same broken expressions. We're all scared and unable to understand why our own bodies are rebelling against us. I can't watch it anymore. Placing my headphones deep in my ears, I lose myself in a few episodes of *Sons of Anarchy* before I doze off.

The next thing I know, Mom gently shakes me awake as Nurse Monroe disconnects my lines, using alcohol swabs on me again.

"Time to go, baby," Mom says as she tucks my blanket back into the bag. It takes both her and Nurse Monroe to help me out of the chair and back onto my feet. With Nurse Monroe steadying me, Mom heads down to get car while I slowly walk toward the door. I hate how weak I feel after my treatments. It's as if my entire body gets the blue screen of death that everyone dreads seeing on their computer and you're left waiting impatiently for it to reboot so you know it will work again. Each step is agonizing to take as my muscles constrict and fight against the poison now flowing through my veins.

It's in these moments that I am also mentally weak, and those dark thoughts are only compounded more with each painful step and disgusting churn of my stomach as it fights to hold in what I had for breakfast. Some people are lucky to feel well after chemo and not have to deal with the side effects for a few days, but I'm not one of the lucky ones. Maybe it's nerves, or the fact that I have never had a strong stomach, but as soon as the port was disconnected, I felt as if a Mack Truck ran my ass over and backed up, only to do it again. Just another reason why I hate having to go through this at all.

Exiting the doors of the chemotherapy room, I take a seat in one of the waiting room chairs and sob uncontrollably. How has my life spiraled so far out of control? I'm not supposed to be sick and fighting for my life at twenty-one. I should be out doing stupid shit, and making bad decisions that I will regret the next day. I should be drinking way too much and streaking through the quad. But, that's not the life that I, Abigail Lynn Brewer, get to live. Instead, I get my boobs hacked off and replaced with a pair of shiny new implants, followed by a medication that is slowly killing my immune system.

*I can't do this anymore.*

I know I'm supposed to be strong. I have the support of all my family and friends, but I hate what I've become. My strength seems to have left the day my doctor uttered the dreaded "C" word. I feel like a failure to the values my dad instilled in me growing up. He always told me fear would get me nowhere, and most things in life aren't worth being afraid of, because if it's meant to be, that's how life will go, no matter what we say otherwise. I wish Dad were here with me; I need him and his soothing words so fucking bad right now.

*I just want my life back to the way it was before cancer, and before Daddy died.*

As my sobs continue, something cold touches my hands, and I look up to see a small figure standing in front of me. As I remove my hands from my face and wipe away my tears, a small girl with thin blonde curls frowns up at me.

"Are you okay?" she asks as she moves her hand to cup my cheek. "Why are you crying?"

Watching her stare up at me, the little girl's green eyes return my gaze with a puzzled look.

"Are you sick?" she asks. "My mama told me it's okay to cry when my tummy feels icky. Does your tummy feel icky?"

Her hand on my face gives me such a strange sensation of comfort, just as her words make me smile.

"Yes, my tummy is feeling icky," I reply, finally finding my voice. Her eyes dim slightly as she strokes my cheek with her tiny fingers.

"Yeah, my tummy feels icky after the gross meddys, too. But, Mama says I hafta do it if I wanna go home. I miss my puppy and Bob."

"Who's Bob?" I question as she slowly takes her hand away from my face.

"He's my stuffed moose. Gramma brought him all the way from Alaska. Papaw was 'posed to bring me a real moose, but the plane people said he was too big to fly."

Quiet laughter escapes my lips as I think about a moose being forcibly shoved onto a plane.

"What's your name?" she inquires. "My name is Cassie Mae Snow.

30

"Well, Cassie Mae Snow, my name is Abby."

Her eyes light up once more. "Ohhhhh. Your name is so purdy."

"Thank you, Cassie. How old are you?"

Holding up three fingers, she waves them in my face. "I'm this many. One. Two. Three. I'm three years old. How old are you?"

"I'm twenty–one."

"You're old like my gramma. She's twenty gazillion years old. Papaw said that when Gramma was born, she got to play with dinozors."

For the first time in nearly two months, I let out a real, from the heart laugh. Cassie giggles along with me, just as two nurses appear on each side of her.

"It's time to go, Cassie. Dr. Katie has you all set up in your favorite pink chair."

Turning to the nurses, she reaches out and places her hands into their much larger ones.

"Didja 'member to find *Bubble Guppies* on the 'puter? I'm 'posed to get to watch my guppies today. I wanna see Bubble Puppy get into trouble with Bubble Kitty again."

The nurses smile down at her as they walk to the chemo room. She turns back from the doors and waves at me.

"Bye, Abby!" she gleefully yells out. Turning back to the nurses, she giggles again and, just as the door closes, I hear her tell the nurses something I never expected out of someone I just met.

"Abby's gonna be my bestest friend."

# Chapter four

Four days after my encounter with the little ray of sunshine that is Cassie, I can't get her out of my head. I'm not sure if it's the beautiful little smile that was plastered on her face, or her courageous spirit, but for the first time in a long time, I am happy when Mom wakes me up even though I know I have to get ready for chemotherapy. My happiness doesn't come from the fact that I will be one treatment closer to being finished, but the idea I might run into Cassie again. Vivid images of her smiling face, and imaginary moments of spending time with her, fly through my thoughts.

This is absolutely crazy. Hell, maybe the poison that has been pumped into my body has finally started to affect my brain, and that's why I feel this pull to see a little girl that I had only spoken to for five minutes. Even as I hurled my guts out the first two days after my last treatment, followed by a third day of muscle pain, I could still picture her smile in my head. I don't understand why, but for some crazy reason, it made the pain a little more bearable.

Mom helps me dress quicker than usual, and before I'm even fully awake, she's loaded me into the car where we head toward the hospital. Once in the parking lot, I nearly bolt out from the car before Mom has it in park.

*What the hell is wrong with me?*

"Where's the fire, Abby?" Mom questions. "I figured today would be like pulling teeth to get you ready for chemo."

I stop and turn back to see her having to jog to keep up with me.

"I don't know why, but I can't get that little girl from my last treatment out of my head. It's crazy, right?"

She finally catches up with me and puts a reassuring hand on my shoulder. "No, baby, it's not weird. Sometimes people like her come into our lives at the right time. I think it would be good for you to see her again, and maybe get to know her. She needs a distraction just as much as you do right now."

"I know, but we've barely spoken. How do I just go up to her family and tell them I'd like to get to know their sick kid? Isn't that a little creepy?"

Mom smirks back at me and shakes her head. "You are both sick, and probably understand more about what's going on than anyone else around you. Why don't you ask Nurse Monroe about her today? See what you can find out, and if you still feel a pull to talk to her, we'll see if her family would be okay with it."

"You know, Mom, you're way smarter than me sometimes."

She smiles again and elbows me in the arm. "You didn't just get your good looks from your mama, baby girl."

We link arms and walk into the elevator. Once we stop at our floor, the doors open, and I take a deep breath before stepping into the hallway.

Peering down the corridor, my shoulders slump in disappointment. There's no sign of Cassie in the halls. I wonder if she doesn't have to have treatments as often as I do, which of course, would complicate things even more. I'll have to work to find out where she might be, if she is still even in the hospital.

Hitting the buzzer on the door, Nurse Monroe comes out to greet us and walks us into the poison den, or so I decided to call it after spending twelve hours hurling in the days after my last visit. I scan the room as we walk to my normal spot, and repeat the usual routine; swab, blood draw, swab, poison injection. Same shit, different day.

Mom hands me my iPad, but nothing I try to watch or read keeps my attention for long. Just as I try to shut my eyes to fall asleep, a familiar little voice calls out my name.

"Mama, looky. It's Abby! She's my new bestest friend. Hi, Abby!" she squeals. "Can I sit next to Abby today?" She looks to her nurse.

"As long as Abby's okay with a little company, I don't see why not, honey child."

Nodding my head in excitement, Cassie rushes over to me and leans over the arm of the chair to see what's on my tablet.

"Where's the toons, Abby? You hafta watch toons when it's meddy time," she says with a smile. "Do you like *Puppy Power Squad*?"

I can't help but smile at her energy and excitement. "You know what? I've never seen it. Do you want to watch it with me, Cassie? I bet I can find it online."

"Duh, Abby. Bestest friends are 'posed to watch toons together."

The nurse that came in with Cassie directs her to the chair next to me as her mom settles into the chair beside her. Cassie's little body is hooked up, and before they turn on the infusion machine, she leans over as far as she can and intently watches the cartoon on the screen.

"I like the spotted puppy. He's my favorite. What's yours?"

"I think I like the spotted puppy, too. He has cool hats."

"Yep," she says with a giggle. "He likes to play pwetend, just like me."

"What do you pretend to be? A ballerina? A teacher? Maybe someone who helps animals?"

36

Cassie rolls her eyes at me and laughs. "You're silly, Abby. That stuff's for babies. I wanna be a basketball pwayer when I grow up. You know, like those guys in the blue shirts that Daddy always yells at on TV. Right, Mama?"

Her mom smiles and nods in agreement. "Her dad loves the Pacers, and she's watched every game with him since she was born. I swear, the day we found out we were having a baby, my husband, Mike, bought anything that had to do with the Pacers for the baby. I'm surprised Cassie's first words weren't, 'Boom, baby!'"

"Booooooooooooooooooom baby," Cassie squeals in delight as her mother tries to shush her. She shrugs her shoulders at her mom's stern look before turning back to me.

"I'm not 'posed to do that."

"It's okay, Cassie. What would you say if I told you I was a basketball player at Purdue?"

"Weallllly? You play basketball? Do you know Bobby Knight? Daddy hates that guy. He's grumpy."

I laugh out loud, while Cassie looks at me in confusion.

"Bobby Knight was the coach at the school my school doesn't like. I'd get in trouble for saying his name at my school," I confide.

"Oh? So it would be like saying a bad word?"

"Yes, just like that. I'd get in big trouble if I said his name at school."

Cassie sits quietly as the nurses check her lines, wincing a few times. While she is distracted, I really take her in. Her blonde curls are even thinner than the last time I saw her, and she looks smaller as well. But, her spirit seems as vivacious as ever. It is baffling to see someone so young, and so gravely ill, be so lively.

The nurse walks away, and Cassie returns her attention to me.

"Can you teach me to play basketball, Abby? I wanna know how to shoot hoops so I can play with Daddy and my bwudder."

"You bet I can. You know what? How would you like it if I try to find one of those hoops that you can hang on the back of your door? That way, if I stop by to see you, we can play. Would you like that?"

Her face lights up like the sky on the Fourth of July.

"Can we watch more *Puppy Power Squad* now?"

"Of course we can."

Flicking my finger across the screen, I pull up the next episode and click play. Cassie leans over and watches the episode, giggling when the puppies on the cartoon do something silly. Four episodes later, Cassie grows quiet and drifts off to sleep. Her mother gently pulls a blanket around her tiny body and lays a soft kiss on her forehead. Cassie doesn't move from the contact of her mother as her chest rises and falls.

"Can I talk to you?" I whisper to her mother. She nods and slips into the chair my mom had previously occupied before leaving to grab some lunch. Mom always argues with me, but it's so unfair for her to sit here hungry as I am confined to this chair.

"I want to make sure it's okay that I have taken an interest in Cassie," I start. "I know in this day and age, you have to be careful who is around your kids, but I promise you, I have no nefarious reasons other than to get to know your little ray of sunshine that barreled into my life."

Cassie's mother reaches out to touch my hand while giving me a bright smile. I'm starting to see where Cassie gets those special smiles from.

"I know you don't have ill intentions for my daughter, Abby. To be frank, it's almost a relief Cassie has connected with you so quickly. She's usually quite shy around strangers, but she gravitated toward you when she saw you crying in the hall. I've honestly never seen her react to someone like that before."

"It was a bit different, wasn't it?" I question. "I have to admit, from the moment she touched me, this sense of calm took me over, and the doubts I had instantaneously vanished. In those few moments, she managed to vanquish all the demons in my life that had consumed me for the last two months."

Her mother gazes at her daughter with tear-filled, loving eyes as she squeezes my hand. "You have no idea how much it hurts to see her so sick, yet with you, it's as if she's back to her old goofy self. We've spent nine out of the last eleven months in this hospital, and every day, her light was dimming, until she saw you. She's been this bright and bubbly little girl ever since you met her in the hallway. You've been this silent, hidden blessing to us, Abby. You've given us our little girl back."

Tears well in my eyes, matching her mother's, as we both watch Cassie sleeping next to us. I know it may not be my place to ask about her condition, but I can't help myself. It's as if I need to know everything I can about her, and my mind is filled with so many questions that they spill out all at once.

"What kind of cancer does she have? Is it treatable?" I blurt out in quick succession without engaging my brain to mouth filter system.

Her mother's hopeful smile fades instantly, and my heart nearly stops beating.

"It's bad, isn't it?" I choke out. "You don't have to tell me. It was presumptuous of me to even ask. I'm sorry, Mrs. Snow. I don't mean to pry."

Her mother's tears fall faster down her face.

"No, it's okay … and please, call me Mary. If you want to be a part of her life, then you need to know what she's facing. Cassie has a form of brain cancer called Diffuse Intrinsic Pontine Glioma, or DIPG. It is very aggressive, and causes tumors to grow at the base of her brain. Cassie's had fifteen surgeries to remove tumors in the last year alone."

My heart, in one single instant, shatters. How can someone so small be forced to endure this kind of medical turmoil? She should be out playing, pretending in the yard with her imaginary friends, not spending her days cooped up in a stuffy hospital with poison being pumped into her tiny little body. This isn't fair at all. It's things like this that make me question how cruel the world can be sometimes.

"Are the treatments helping at all?"

Her mother, Mary, breaks down, and I grip her hand tightly, trying to comfort her the only way I know how. Her chest heaves sorrowfully with each heart-wrenching sob.

"Cassie has been on experimental treatments for the last three months, and they aren't working anymore," Mary says while looking at her daughter. "I'm so afraid we are going to lose my sweet girl, and I'd give anything, including my own life, to make sure she lives."

Anger begins to course through my veins. Cassie shouldn't be on the brink of death at three years old. As many would turn to religion in a time like this, I can't help but cast doubt on why God would cut someone's life so short. It's not Cassie's time. She has way too much to live for and experience. Three years on Earth is just not enough.

"How long?" I ask.

"Six months to a year, if we are lucky. Her doctor has already spoken to us about hospice care, and making arrangements for her ahead of time. I just can't fathom having to do this for our little girl. She can't be leaving us. There are so many things our family didn't get to do with her."

I cry alongside Mary for nearly an hour. Cassie begins to stir as the nurse starts to unhook her and me from our lines. Cassie quietly sobs in her drowsy state, whimpering for her mother. Mary rushes to her side and caresses her blonde curls as Cassie begins to cry about not feeling well. Watching her and her mother, I know I need to help this little girl make some of her dreams come true. I can't let the world lose someone like Cassie without first giving her a chance to really live.

Just as the nurses help place Cassie onto a hospital bed, I quietly call out to Mary, "Would it be okay if I visit her in a few days?"

Her mother nods her head as the gurney is wheeled out of the room. "She's in room 303."

"I'll be by as soon as I can," I call out.

Mom saunters in, just as Nurse Monroe finishes the last swab and helps me gather my things.

As we make our way to the car, my mind races with ideas of what I can do to help make Cassie's dreams come true when an idea so crazy, and so impossible, flitters to reality.

"Can you dig out my phone from my bag, Mom? I need to call Coach Beck."

"Why, baby? You can't go back to playing yet. Besides, it's the off-season," she says as she helps me into the car.

I wave her off from buckling my seatbelt and wait for her to slide into the driver's seat before I explain.

"That's not it, Mom. Please just give me my phone."

She digs around in my backpack and pulls out it out, tossing it into my lap before she starts the car. I fumble to pick it up, then quickly unlock it with my fingerprint as I begin to scroll for Coach Beck's number. Once I find it, I click on her name and wait.

The phone rings five times before a gruff voice answers.

"Beck," is all the voice says as a greeting.

"Coach, it's Abby. I need your help with something."

# chapter five

The next nine weeks are a complete and utter blur of spending every free second I can with Cassie between both of our treatment schedules. At one point, her nurses asked if I was planning on moving into her room after my treatments ended. Cassie, of course, thinks that is a great idea, and spends six straight hours telling me about how our "woom," is going to be decorated. According to her and her wild imagination, our room will be hot pink and teal, with moose and basketballs all over the walls. With her hands on those bossy little hips of hers, she also informs me that I will only be able to play with her toys when she says I can.

Just thinking about the wild conversations she and I have had in the last few weeks brings an instant smile to my lips. This cherub-faced little girl has brought back so much joy to my life. I know the surprise I have planned for her will let her know how much I care about her. Yet, all of our time together hasn't been as happy as it should be.

It wasn't until the last three weeks that things began to worsen. Mary was fired from her job after using up all her family medical leave, and Mike, Cassie's dad, returned to work to keep their family afloat, while making sure Cassie's brother, Mason, still made it to school and his other activities. Mary desperately clung to the small paychecks she received from her high school secretary job, but now, their financial woes and decreased income have become tight nooses around their necks. Every trip they make back and forth to the hospital costs them nearly a hundred dollars in gas, but Mary will not miss a single day to be there for Cassie at the hospital. I began spending the night from time to time, allowing Cassie's family a break from the uncomfortable chairs. I wanted to allow them to get a good night's rest in their own beds, and helping conserve their costs in gas. It kills me inside to watch her parents worry over the financial aspects of her treatment.

On top of the financial strain now facing her family, Cassie's health has begun to decline far more rapidly than even her doctors had expected. She and I went from playing basketball with the little basket I brought for her and giggling the night away, to spending most of the time lying in her bed, watching TV and barely talking. Her voice became raspier and raspier as her talking moved from constant to sporadic. She went from a vibrant, energetic child to one who barely left her bed for more than a few, fleeting minutes. It brings tears to my eyes to think of one of the very last conversations we had before her health started to decline.

*"Abby? When you go back to school and play basketball, will you stop coming to see me?"*

*Shock must have registered on my face, because Cassie frowned.*

*"Why would you think I wouldn't want to spend time with you? You are my best friend, Cassie. I'll always want to spend time with you."*

*"You will?"*

*"Of course I will. I can't play without my favorite fan cheering me on in the crowd. There's no way I could play without you."*

*"Even if I can't be there, how will I know you're thinkin' about me when you're playing basketball?"*

*Thinking on her insightful question, an idea popped into my head. Holding up three fingers, like she did the first time we met, I pressed them against my heart.*

*"When I do this," I say, wiggling my fingers against my chest. "It will be our sign. It's my way of letting you know that I'm thinking about you, and that I'll see you soon."*

*Cassie mimicked my gesture. "We don't need bestest fwiend neckwaces, do we?"*

*"No, Cassie. We don't need something hanging around our necks to show that we're best friends."*

46

The sudden realization that I am losing one of the most important people in my life hits me like a speeding train coming off its tracks. I'm not ready to lose her, and I know with her time growing short, I have to push the timetable up on our surprise. I'm not about to let Cassie's light dim to nothingness without giving her a happy memory to think about.

It took so many people to coordinate what I have planned, but as of last night, the final piece finally fell into place. Her doctors fought hard against me, saying it would put her under unnecessary stress, but they finally agreed once her condition began to worsen. She deserves to have a dream granted, and today is the day little Cassie Mae Snow will get her wish.

Pulling up to the hospital, I know today will be a key point in her little life, and I want it to be perfect. Sliding from the seat of my car into the hot Indiana summer sun, I look behind me to make sure everyone is in place. Waving to a few of my fellow conspirators to follow me, we start our trek to her room.

Stopping just short of the door, I halt the group behind me.

"I'm going to go in and see how she's doing first. I'll let you guys know when it's time to come in."

The group nods their heads in unison as I step inside. Cassie is lying on her large bed, staring out the window in her room, with her stuffed moose tucked tightly against her body. I knock quietly, and her face immediately turns to me. Cassie smiles and waves for me to come over.

47

Sitting at her bedside, she hugs me and lays her head against my side.

"How is my bestest friend today?" I ask, knowing the chance at hearing an answer isn't likely. She nods her head and smiles, holding me tighter.

"She was up and down most of the night last night," Mary informs me. "She did manage to eat a good breakfast, though. She put away four pieces of bacon and three scrambled eggs."

Looking back down at Cassie, she nods her head again. "Holy Moly, Cassie Mae. You ate more than I did for breakfast!" I exclaim joyfully. Cassie hasn't eaten that much in nearly a month for a single meal, so I know that has given Mary some comfort.

"Well, it's a good thing you had a big breakfast, because you're going to need all your energy today, Miss Cassie Mae."

She peers up at me with a puzzled expression.

"What if I told you I brought you a little surprise?"

Her eyes light up with excitement for the first time in what seems like forever.

"Do you want to see what your surprise is?"

She nods her head, and I call out to the people in the hall.

One by one, they enter the room, and Cassie's eyes look to each person, then look to her mother, and finally, she looks at me with a tiny trail of tears falling from her eyes.

"Cassie, I would like for you to meet a few of my friends. This is Lauren, Madison, Gabby, and our coach, Kyla Beck, from my basketball team at school." The girls and Coach Beck each wave and say their hellos to both Cassie and her mom, but I notice Cassie's eyes are now locked onto the tallest person she's likely ever seen.

"Now, if you've watched basketball with your daddy, you know who that is," I say, pointing to the tall man behind the girls. Her eyes grow wide.

"Cassie, I would like to introduce you to Paul Turner. Can you say hello?"

Cassie gives him a wave as Paul approaches her bedside.

"Well, it's good to meet you, Cassie. Abby here tells me you really like basketball, and the Pacers are your favorite team. Is that right?"

Cassie's eyes light up like diamonds on a clear night sky as she quietly whispers, "Uh huh."

"Well, what if I told you that Abby has another surprise waiting for you outside? Would you like to go see it?"

Cassie squeezes me even tighter and looks to her mother, her eyes pleading for her to say yes.

"Cassie, baby, Mommy's already said you can go. Would you like that?"

Nodding, she bounces on her bed ever so slightly.

"Well, if that's a yes, I think you might want to put this on," says Paul, while handing her a Pacers jersey with her name on the back.

Cassie grabs the jersey from his hands and stares at the sight in front of her before throwing up her hands for help to put it on. Mary hits the button on the bed to call the nurses. After a few moments, the nurses enter the room to help us unhook Cassie's IV so we can go on our adventure. Once unhooked, I help Cassie put on her jersey, just before Paul picks her up in his arms. We follow them out of the room.

Cassie's legs bounce as our group makes its way toward the entrance, where music begins to pour through the hospital's front doors each time they open. Cassie's eyes look so happy as she feels sunshine for the first time in months. She closes her eyes as the bright rays hit her pale face, before nuzzling into Paul's strong arms.

The music begins to get louder and louder, and just as we round the corner, Cassie lets out a gasp.

The Purdue All-American Marching Band stands proudly before us, playing Cassie's favorite song, "Let It Go", from the Frozen soundtrack. Next to the band stands the entire Purdue cheerleading squad, Golden Girl, Silver Twins, and even the Boilermaker Special, with a banner that reads, "Cassie's Caravan," on the side.

Even I stand in awe of the spectacular sight in front of us. I turn to Coach Beck, who smiles in return.

"I don't understand, Coach. How did you pull this off?"

She looks to Cassie's sweet face, who is bobbing along to the music.

"The night you called and asked for help to get one of the Pacers players here wasn't enough. I called in a few favors, and your idea took off from there. You so desperately wanted to make Cassie's dream come true, so myself, and the entire athletic staff, wanted to give you both a day you'll never forget." Heavy tears roll down my face as I hug tightly onto Coach Beck. "You've inspired me, Abby, with what you wanted to do for Cassie, and there's a few more things I need to show you."

"Wait … what? There's more?"

Coach Beck smirks and motions for me to follow her.

"You have no idea what else I have in store for the both of you."

# Chapter
## six

Cassie and I, along with her family and my mom, are directed to load into the back of the Boilermaker Special. After weaving through Lafayette, we cruise down State Road 26 toward the campus, with Disney music blaring from the speakers. Mike, Cassie's dad, looks stunned as he stares at Paul Turner, who is sitting next to his little girl. The look on his face was priceless when he saw who was carrying his daughter outside. I swear, I thought we'd have to turn right around and go back into the hospital to get him treated for shock.

Cassie sits on my lap, covered in a thick blanket to keep her frail body warm. Some cars honk, while others on the streets call out her name as we drive by, which she greets with a little wave. The closer we get to campus, I see ribbons are tied around every light post, and the streets are lined with students, waving banners and posters with, "#Cure4Cassie", written on them. Adjusting Cassie on my lap, I pull out my cell phone from my back pocket and search the hashtag.

One of the trending topics on the ESPN Sports Nation website is #Cure4Cassie. How in the hell did they even know about this? I scroll through pages and pages, all mentioning the hashtag, on so many social media sites. My heart swells with each place I see the support for Cassie, and their outpouring of love for their family. But, it's the very last page I click on that breaks the flood gates.

Someone had placed Cassie's story on a fundraiser site, and there, in brightly-colored letters, is a number that shocks me to the core—*two hundred seventy-five thousand dollars*. Complete strangers, people who had only read about her story in a few paragraphs on the page, blessed her family beyond words during a desperate time in their lives. Holding out my phone to her parents, Mary and Mike take in what the screen reads and they both start to cry, clinging to each other as they say quiet blessings toward the heavens. I can't help but squeeze Cassie just a little tighter.

But, the moment of joy is nothing compared to what waits for us once our ride on the Boilermaker Special concludes. The Reamer Club members, who had been our drivers for this leg of the trip, hop out of the cab and open the front doors of Mackey Arena. Paul exits first, helping

Mike and Mary out before Mike leans back inside to lift Cassie from my lap.

As the doors open, a low rumble of noise begins to pour out of the court area. Cassie's eyes light up as we are ushered toward the locker rooms and court entrance areas that I call home. As we step into the tunnel for the court, both sides are lined by the athletic staff, the men's basketball team, and my own teammates, clapping and cheering for Cassie. Slapping their hands as we walk by, we step out onto the court as the crowd cheers loudly.

Turning to look up into the stands, every single seat is filled with fans wearing a pink shirt with the number three, chanting Cassie's name. Her family rotates to take in the scene before them. Cassie slowly claps along to the most joyful noise I have ever heard, then a microphone is tapped, bringing our attention back to the court.

Coach Beck stands at center court with the entire Pacers team at her sides. Each man towers over Coach Beck as she beckons us to the floor. Cassie's little arms reach for me, and her father hands her over. Together, Cassie and I step onto my home court as the crowd roars even louder, if that's even possible.

"Ladies and Gentlemen, please welcome number three to Keady Court, Cassie Mae Snow!" yells our regular game announcer.

"We have a surprise for you, Cassie. Abby told me you wanted to be able to watch her play basketball, and even though it's the off-season, we're going to make that happen. Our Lady Boilers are going to play on this very court against you and your dad's favorite team. What do you think about that, Cassie?"

She beams from ear to ear as she claps in excitement. I wish I could hear her little voice cheer as it once did, but just seeing her as happy as she is right now is all I need.

"Who's ready to Boiler Up and play for Cassie?" Coach bellows into the microphone.

The fans begin to stomp and clap as our team entrance music begins to boom from the speakers with the Purdue P lights rotating over the crowd. The slow claps to the music shake the foundation of Mackey as Coach Beck welcomes the teams to the court. Every player comes to Cassie and high fives her as they warm-up on the floor.

Britney, one of our assistant coaches, directs us to the home bench. Cassie settles into my lap and watches the game from the front row. Just before the second half ends, Coach Beck approaches me and holds out my jersey to Cassie.

"Don't you think it's time for Abby to show you her stuff, Cassie?"

Cassie claps as her dad moves to take her from me. Slipping my jersey over my head, I step onto the black and gold hardwood of Keady Court as a player for the first time since my diagnosis. Madison feeds me the ball on an inbound throw, and I run straight into the tall man in front of me to lay it up. As the ball circles the rim before sinking into the net, I look over to Cassie to see her eyes locked onto mine, and I press my three fingers against my chest. I play my heart out for her, and as the final buzzer sounds,

I run back to Cassie and scoop her back into my arms. We step out onto the court as I hand her the game ball.

"So, what did you think? Did you like watching me play?"

Her raspy voice whispers into my ear, "I love you, Abby."

"I love you too, Cassie Mae," I whisper back as I hug her. We get lost in the crowd and the energy of Mackey.

A short time later, Cassie's parents load her into their car to go back to the hospital. I watch as she drives away with the basketball gripped tightly on her lap, and our sign against her chest.

I'm walking on cloud nine, knowing Cassie's dream was finally achieved, but a late phone call that night changed everything. In a single instance, the joy that swelled within my heart turns to sadness and worry as Mary sobs into the phone, unable to speak clearly.

"It's Cassie. You need to come to the hospital, Abby."

# Chapter seven

Standing in front of the mirror at my apartment, I take a long, hard look at myself. After months of chemo and the side effects that came with it, I look like the dead ghost of my former self. My skin is pale and translucent, with the dark blue veins drawing a road map under my skin. My battle with cancer has seemed to age me far worse than I could have ever imagined. Running my fingers through the soft stubble of my hair, the memory of my long hair brings tears to my eyes.

"You look so beautiful." Cassie had told me when I cried over the loss of my hair. "You are my twin now, okay?" Her cute little smile lit up as she ran her fingers over the smoothness of my head.

After the call from Mary the night of her surprise basketball game, I never left her room until her little eyes closed for the last time, four days later. As her family grieved, I quietly snuck out of the room and left the hospital. My time with Cassie had come to a close, and I didn't want to intrude on her family any more than I already had.

I said my last goodbyes to her from the doorway of her room as her family lie strewn across her bed, begging her for one last word or one last breath, not wanting to believe she was gone. I couldn't admit to them that I was relieved that she finally found peace, and that she was with the "Purdy Angels" she always talked about seeing in her dreams, so it was better that I left them to mourn as a family.

Deep down, I had always wondered when she talked about dreaming of the angels, that she may not have been dreaming at all. Perhaps Cassie was getting a glimpse of Heaven. That's one of the funny things about the afterlife. You really don't know if it's real until you pass from this Earth, but even as skeptical as I have been during portions of my life, I know that little Miss Cassie Mae Snow is running around Heaven, sharing those bright smiles and making everyone so damn happy. One day, if I am lucky, I will get to see her again.

While I had already said my goodbyes the night she died, she wasn't through with me yet. Just a few days after her passing, a text came from Mary, asking if she could call me. I hesitated at first, but I agreed to talk.

During our brief conversation, I discovered that Cassie had made one request for after she went to see the angels. She wanted her mom to make sure that I came to see her one last time, and to give me a box she had been working on for my birthday. I told Mary that I didn't know if I would be strong enough to come to the funeral, and she understood my reasoning, but she politely asked that I see what Cassie's box contained before I made a decision. I agreed and met up with her later that evening at Starbucks, after basketball practice, for the exchange. She hugged me and said she hoped she would see me at the services the next morning before handing me the box and walking back to her car.

It took three hours before I could lift the lid of the box to see what Cassie had left for me, but when I did, I found dozens of hand-drawn pictures and cards, and, after reading each one, Cassie's love for me took another chunk out of the armor I had placed around my heart the night she died. But, it wasn't until the last one that I broke. It wasn't a card, but a small book made of stapled construction paper. She had drawn our adventures together, each page filled with memories from wheelchair racing to the night Cassie walked out onto Keady Court with me and the crowd cheering for her.

But, the last page was something completely different. Cassie had drawn us both with long hair and smiles on our faces, but while she had drawn me on the ground, she was flying with the angels, three little fingers pressed to her heart. With that one picture, Cassie made me realize just how much I was going to miss her, and how much her family needed me there with them as they said their goodbyes. They needed me like I needed her.

Wiping the tears from my face, I straighten my simple, tea-length, black dress and glance at the clock. Stepping out of my room, I pick up my purse and leave my apartment. The drive to the funeral home is short, but at the same time, it feels like the longest ride of my life.

As I pull into the parking lot, one of the attendants asks me my name and directs me where to park. As I pull in behind a blue MINI, I realize I am the second car in line. Weren't the spots in front of the procession usually reserved for family members? Before I can ask, the same attendant who checked me in, quietly opens my car door and helps me out.

Walking up the cobblestone steps, another attendant opens the door and ushers me into the waiting area. I wander for several minutes in the lobby, looking at the flowers and photos her family had selected of Cassie to display. Each photo brings tears to my eyes as I learn about the things she was able to do before cancer took its hold on her life. I never knew she went to Disney World, or that she had fallen asleep in her car seat using two loaves of bread as pillows. There is so much about her that I never got to know about, and it kills me that the only memories I have of her will be from the damn hospital and our one night of freedom together.

Stepping into the line for the room holding Cassie's casket, I wait for my turn to take a seat. As the line slowly moves, I begin to slide into the back row when one of the attendants taps me on the shoulder and escorts me to the very last seat in the front. I try to protest, but Mary quickly reaches over and grabs my hand.

"Cassie loved you like a sister, and your place is with us, Abby. You may not be our daughter by blood, but you have become a daughter to us in spirit, and the love you shared for our little Cassie."

I instantly pull her into a tight embrace as we begin to cry. A quiet hush falls over the room as a young minister steps to the front of the full room.

"I could stand in front of you today and read scriptures about how we should trust God's reasons for calling Cassie home, but her family has prepared a short video."

He steps to the side as a screen in the front corner of the funeral home blinks to life. Cassie Mae Snow scrolls across the screen, then pictures set to music fade in and out. Videos ranging from the day she was born, to her first three birthdays, begin to play as a soft country ballad plays in the background. But, it's the last video that stuns me. Cassie's smiling in my arms as we walk onto the basketball court while the crowd roars and chants her name. The video pauses with our two faces staring and smiling back at each other as the chants continue, then the video fades to black.

The minister returns to the front of the room as the video ends and wipes away his own tears.

"I would now like to invite those who wish to speak, share a memory, or maybe even a song, to please stand as you are able." One by one, Cassie's relatives stand and share memories of her. As each person sits, the minister begins to speak again.

"If there's no one else, then—"

"I would like to say something, if that's okay," I interrupt. He nods his head for me to continue, so I turn to face the room.

"Cassie was my hero. Until I met her, I never felt like a person in the hospital, just another patient with orders to be filled. Every day in that hospital was a prison sentence, and I was just another prisoner waiting for the day I would be set free from my cell. But, Cassie never felt like that. She made the best of the situation, and tried to make everyone smile. The day I met Cassie, I had just had my second chemo treatment. I sat in a chair outside the chemotherapy room and cried. I cried because of the pain I was in and for other selfish reasons. A small little girl sidled up to me and put her hands on my face. She told me that she wanted to make me feel better, and gave me this thousand megawatt smile that I swear could light up an entire city. She hugged me, a complete stranger, and for the first time, I had hope. I felt if a little girl like her could smile while facing this disease, so could I.

"As the treatments continued, I looked forward to seeing her, and to hear her silly stories about the crazy stuffed moose in her room and what it did to the nurses. Cassie had so much life left in her, and it kills me to know that she's not here to brighten my day anymore. I may have beaten breast cancer, but Cassie triumphed over her own battle. She made every day worth living, and even at the end, she passed with a sweet smile on her face. I know that she is looking down on us now, and every time I feel the sun on my face, I know it's her smiling down on me.

"Cassie wouldn't want us to mourn her. She would want each and every one of us to make each day we get on this Earth special—to smile for those who can't, and to give hope to those who are lost. On one of the worst days of my life, her sweet little voice told me that every tummy ache was worth it because she got to be my friend. She called me her angel on Earth because I made her dreams come true. What Cassie didn't know was that she was *my* angel. She saved me, by teaching me how to look at the world with a child's eyes, and see the wonders that surround us. Life may not always be a forever thing, but for her, it was worth every single day she fought cancer. May you all be as blessed by her spirit as I was, and I hope every day you can find a reason to give the world one of her megawatt smiles. It may just save someone's life."

As the last word leaves my lips, I slowly descend back into my seat and sob into my hands. The minister requests that those who would like to say their final goodbyes do so at this time. Each person walks past her casket, offering condolences to her family. Her parents, grandparents, and brother, stand up next to me as we surround her casket. We stand as one, like a family, and look down at our precious little Cassie. Mary looks to me and nods, then leads her family out of the room, giving me a moment alone to say one last, final, goodbye.

"I love you, Cassie," I whisper just before I lay a gentle kiss on her cold forehead. I step away from her casket and turn to exit the room. I take in massive displays of flower arrangements, lighted angels, and prayer blankets as I walk toward the door and stop to look back at her one last time. That's when something catches my eye, making me stop in my tracks.

At the very last table, next to the door, is a single lighted angel with my name on the card. Walking back inside, I make my way to the card, flipping it over to see who it is from.

*Just like me, this angel will light up your life. Love, Cassie.*

I nearly fall to my knees in tears as the pallbearers enter the room. I know I can't linger, so I quickly exit the room. As the doors close behind me, I stop and press my three fingers to my heart and silently say my last goodbye to the only person I knew who loved unconditionally.

# epilogue

## Six Months Later

"Are you ready?" Coach Beck screams into the locker room. "Tonight is our night! This is our court in our arena, and that is our trophy!" She points to the display case holding the Barn Burner Trophy that has been ours for the last six years. My teammates rally behind the coach's words, hootin' and hollerin' right along with her.

"It's been a tough season, but we have prevailed. For some of you, it's the last time you will step out onto Keady Court and play in this arena. Play your hearts out, and leave every last ounce of Boilermaker spirit and pride on the hardwood. Now, let's get out there and show those Hoosiers who this state belongs to!"

One by one, our team files out with our coaches to the tunnel that leads to the arena. The music is rattling the walls of the tunnel as our team huddles up one last time.

"Like Coach said," I yell over the noise. "This is our night and our time. No one can take this moment away from us, and if they try, we'll show them exactly why we are Boilermakers. Be Strong. Be Smart. Be Invincible," I scream. The band begins to play "Hail Purdue", and the announcer welcomes us to the floor. Our team bolts from the tunnel and runs onto the court as the sold-out crowd stands and cheers our entrance. Running by the miniature version of the Boilermaker Special, I ring the Extra Special's bell and watch as my teammates take control of the floor.

We shoot around and warm-up for twenty minutes before settling into the sidelines. All I can think about as I prepare to play my last game in my home arena is how much I wish Cassie were here in the stands to see this. She would have loved the excitement and electricity flowing from the crowd. Looking behind the bench, I can picture her in my mind, waving her little black and gold pom-poms with a cheerleading uniform on. Cassie may have never gotten to see me play in a real game, but the memory of her laughter and smiles during the exhibition game against the Pacers we played just for her will live with me forever, even if that day was far more special than I had ever let on.

The truth is that I've held a secret deep inside that only my family knew about. The morning of Cassie's game, Dr. Bragg had called to tell me I was cancer free. I know I should have been ecstatic at the news, but it was more important for me to celebrate Cassie's fight and spend the first day of remission with her. Not telling Cassie my news was probably going to be one of my biggest regrets, and yet, at the same time, one of the happiest moments in my life. I gave up celebrating my good news to be with her for an adventure, and to see her smile one last time.

Returning my gaze to the court, I watch as my teammates strip off their warm-ups. Lauren and Maddy smile at me as they pull theirs over their heads, and plastered right on the front of their jerseys is the number three. Seeing all my other teammates also wearing the same jerseys with the number three, I stand in shock.

"Why is everyone wearing Cassie's number?" I ask as I take in the scene in front of me.

"It's not just us, Cassie." Lauren points across the court. "Look." Following the direction she's pointing in, the crowd begins to cheer. IU's entire team is clapping for us, and their jerseys also have a three.

The crowd roars to life as they begin to chant the number with three fingers placed over their hearts; Cassie's and my sign. Walking farther out onto the court, my eyes scan the crowd, and I realize it's not just the teams with Cassie's number. The entire stadium is wearing bright pink shirts with her number on them, too.

"Abby, I need you to meet me on center court," Coach Beck says to me over the cheering. I follow her, and after I look to the center of the court, I see Cassie's parents and little brother standing on the large P next to something covered in a black cloth. Coach Beck shakes each of their hands, and Mary opens her arms to me. I run to her and hug her tightly as Mike and Mason join in.

Someone hands Coach Beck a microphone.

"As most of you know, Abby here fought a brave battle with breast cancer. While she survived, there is someone who is not with us tonight. While in the hospital, Abby met a three-year-old girl named Cassie. This amazing little girl not only staked a claim on Abby's heart, but on our hearts as well. We lost Cassie nearly six months ago, and though she is gone, her spirit has kept this team going through some of the hardest games this season. We have asked Cassie's parents, Mary and Mike, along with her brother, Mason, to join us tonight. While we know that we can't bring Cassie back, we want to give her family back a tiny piece of what she gave us."

Coach Beck turns to Cassie's family and smiles. "On behalf of the Purdue and IU Women's Basketball programs, along with the Purdue Center for Cancer Research, we would like to bestow upon you a gift." Coach Beck pulls off the black cloth, revealing a child size jersey with Cassie's name on the back, and her number sewn into the mesh.

"We have decided that Cassie gave our team such hope while Abby faced breast cancer that we needed to have a piece of her here in Mackey Arena. This jersey will be hung from the rafters of this arena. Cassie will not only be in our hearts, but here in spirit as well."

Cassie's parents weep as we come together in a loving embrace once more.

"But, that is not all we have for you today. Enclosed in this envelope is three season passes for your family to sit in a place of honor behind our bench for life, which we have now officially named Cassie's Corner."

The crowd roars to life as they begin to chant Cassie's name. Tears stream down my face, and for the first time in a long time, I can feel Cassie's spirit. I know that while she may not be here, she is looking down on us all, smiling that beautiful smile, and holding those three little fingers to her chest, just as I am right now.

I know that tonight was meant to be my last night playing here, but it doesn't feel like it's my night. No, tonight is Cassie's night to shine. It doesn't matter what the final score may be, because Cassie's fight with cancer is more important than any W or L next to our names in the record books. As I walk off the court, listening to the crowd continue to cheer her name, an idea pops into my head.

This court may be named after one of the greatest basketball coaches in college history, but just for tonight, it's Cassie's Court. And I, for one, am proud to have known the most important player in Purdue basketball history, because Cassie is the only person to have ever gone undefeated.

AVELYN PAIGE

**The End**

# A Special Note from the Author

I know many of you may be upset with how this story ended, and trust me, I get it. The lack of a true happily ever after ate me alive as the story developed in my head. No matter how hard I tried to make this into an HEA, that's just not how the characters spoke to me. In thinking about the words I had written as I completed the draft, I realized why this story needed to be told.

Cassie's Court isn't about Abby or Cassie's battle against cancer. It is about the love between two complete strangers, and how much their spirit and love for each other taught them how important it is to experience all life has to offer. Even with three short years of life, Cassie made memories that most of us as adults could we ever had the chance to make. She as a fictional character took the darkness that enveloped her life and turned it into something positive. She strove to help others when she couldn't help herself, and inspired everyone around her. It's with that thought that I wanted to tell you a very personal story.

Cancer has touched so many people in my life. From the age of twelve, I have lost sixteen friends, and family members, to cancer. It was watching one of my closest childhood friends and daily social staples in my life (ironically enough, my school bus driver) pass from bone marrow cancer that really impacted the way I view the world. Marilyn drove my bus every single day, even while taking treatments, and on her last trip before she was too sick to keep working, she stopped me as I exited the bus. She told me that being a good person is one of the best qualities in the world, but to be someone who inspired those around them to fight for others instead of themselves, is a far greater quality. She knew that I was always went to walk a different path from life and that my dreams weren't some childhood fantasy. I could make them real if I tried hard enough.

It wasn't until this year as I watched my own father slip quietly away from a short battle with cancer that I realized how much her words shaped my life. While Marilyn had inspired me to follow a career path in cancer research and attempt to try to find a cure. It was those last words she spoke to me that flittered into my mind when Dad died. He always told me that I was meant for greatness, and while most of us would say that's what all daddies say to their kids, it was a very different meaning for him.

My Dad put his life on the line every single day on the police force for nearly twenty-one years, but it was the relationships he built with his fellow officers and the pride he had for upholding justice and the law that truly set him apart. On the day of his funeral, the police department he helped build, showed our family how much his service meant to the city and them personally. Forty-seven state, local, and city police cars, along with several federal agencies, lined the street of our tiny town to send my father off like the true hero he was. Dad inspired every single officer standing in respect for him that day to be the best officer they could be, and for some, to even be an officer of the law. Seeing these brave men and women mourn alongside our family and honor a fallen hero humbled me, yet inspired me to strive to be as inspiring as he was.

While my dad couldn't be here when my first book was published, I knew he would be proud of the accomplishments I had made in his absence. It's with him in mind that I wrote Damaged, and the reason that I even undertook this story, knowing how much it would wreck me. While this story, for the most part, was fictional, it teaches us all a very important lesson. Hope comes in many forms, and when the world blesses you with one special person, no matter how long they have on this earth, embrace them. Whether you spend years, days, or even minutes together, every second is worth it, and should be cherished. It will be those kind of memories that will make a difference in your life. Strive to inspire those around you, and when it is your turn to need support, take it with open arms, because just like in Cassie and Abby's story, unconditional love will always conquer all.

# Cassie's Wish

### Coming 2017

They say lightning never strikes twice, but Abby Turner is the exception to that rule.

After cancer stole her childhood dream, there was only one bright spot left in Abby's life: Cassie.

But like an executioner wielding a sword, cancer stole her too and forced Abby to watch every brutal moment.

Seven years later, Abby is carrying on Cassie's legacy of helping others when a chance meeting in the hospital cafeteria changes everything. Beau is sweet, kind, and everything Abby has ever wanted.

But darkness is never truly far away, and once more the grim reaper is stalking its prey. Only this time, he doesn't want Abby... He wants Beau.

But this time, Abby is stronger. This time, Abby refuses to back down without a fight.

Her own battle against cancer may be over, but the war has just begun.

Keep Reading for an
Excerpt from:

All That Glitters
By Geri Glenn

# Chapter One

"I'm so very sorry, Miss Brogan."

My entire body is frozen in shock as I stare back at the doctor, unsure exactly what she is trying to say. "Malignant. What does that mean?"

She folds her hands on top of her desk and presses her lips together. "It means the biopsy proved that the lump in your breast is cancer."

I flop back in my seat and my hand flutters to my throat. I fight back the bile and concentrate on taking slow, regular breaths. "What can we do about it?" My voice is strangled and my throat aches as I brace myself for what her answer may be.

"At this stage, I believe that our best course of action is an immediate lumpectomy, followed by an aggressive chemotherapy treatment." A tear slips down my cheek as I sit across from the doctor I've only met with once before, my body trembling in fear. "Miss Brogan, is there someone you'd like me to call? A family member perhaps? You really shouldn't be dealing with this on your own."

I swallow and shake my head, my face set in stone. "No, it's okay. I don't really know anyone in Nashville."

Dr. Begley stands, walks around her desk and perches herself on the edge, directly in front of me. "Where is your family, Kinsley?"

"Canada," I whisper, feeling more alone than I've ever felt.

"I think you should consider doing your treatment in an environment that you will have your loved ones around you." I don't tell her that I only have one loved one—my dad. Other than that, I'm completely alone. "I've went ahead and scheduled your surgery for this coming Thursday. I feel it's best to remove that lump as soon as possible. After that, we can discuss your chemotherapy. If necessary, I can contact a doctor near your family to start the process there."

I swallow down the giant lump I feel forming in my throat and take the appointment slip from her. She gives me a brief pre-operation rundown, but I barely hear what she's saying. When she stands from where she's perched, I take that as my cue to leave and stand as well, shaking her hand and mumbling a brief farewell.

I walk out of the office with my purse clutched to my chest, my pre-op instructions crammed into my fist. I have cancer. I'm only twenty-four years old, and I have cancer.

Stepping out the main door and onto the sidewalk, I am immediately greeted by my driver. I don't know his name because the limo service sends a different one almost every time, and this is the first time I've had this guy. He opens the back door for me without a sound and waits until I'm inside before closing it behind me.

As the car pulls out onto the busy street, I watch the medley of pedestrians as they hurry to their next meeting or appointment, oblivious to the fact that my life has just irrevocably changed. Just when my dream had finally come true too.

Barely a year ago, I'd been playing my guitar at a little coffee shop in Toronto when a music producer had approached me. He'd loved my songs and my voice, and before I knew it, I had a recording contract with one of the biggest country music recording labels in the US, and a fancy new penthouse condo in Nashville. I had just finished recording my first album last week.

It's not fair! Everything was going so good for me. A sob bursts from my chest and I stop fighting back the tears. My body shakes with the force of my cries. I let it all out; my anger, my frustration, my pain, but mostly my fear. What if I can't beat this?

# Chapter Two

"Do you have any idea how much money we've invested in promoting this tour?"

I sit in the chair, watching as Neal Valliant, the record label representative in charge of my contract, paces back and forth in front of the window. "I know, Neal. And I'm so sorry."

He freezes mid-step and turns his head towards me. "Oh, sweetheart, that sounded terrible. I didn't mean it like that at all. You have nothing to be sorry about. I will deal with all of that. Besides, it's not forever, right?" He takes the seat beside me and squeezes my hand. "We'll start planning your tour again once you kick this cancer's ass."

I force a smile and nod.

"When's the surgery?" he asks quietly.

"Tomorrow morning."

"You're going to do great, Kinsley."

My chin quivers a little as I smile sadly at him. The truth is, besides the doctor that gave me the news yesterday, this is the first I've talked to anyone about it. It still doesn't seem real to me. I tried to call my dad, but as usual, he didn't answer. He was likely out fishing, or working in his woodshop. He probably hasn't noticed that I'd even called and left a message.

"This could work to our advantage," Paula says from her chair, off to the left. Her fingers stroke her lips, and you can practically see the wheels spinning as she tries to come up with a way to present this to the public. Paula Quinn is the recording label's publicist, and someone that I have never quite managed to connect with, though I can't really put my finger on what it is about her that I don't like.

"We could make a public statement about your cancer, and follow your journey with bi-weekly updates, photo shoots, and TV interviews. 'Rising country star battles deadly cancer.' The public will eat this up!"

Neal and I exchange a glance, and I can tell from him expression that he disagrees with Paula's idea just as much as I do. I feel like I'm drowning. Ever since I'd gotten the news that I have breast cancer, I've felt like I'm underwater. Now, listening to Paula, I just want to sink to the bottom and be alone. I haven't even had this contract for a year. I have to listen to Paula, and she's saying she wants to turn this whole terrible disease into a money making publicity story.

"I … Paula, I'm really not comfortable with the media being—"

She waves me off and rolls her eyes, as if I'm being silly. "We can talk about all of this later. You worry about taking care of you, darling. Your surgery is tomorrow?"

I stare back at her, my scalp prickling with unease, and nod.

She smiles at me then, and I can't help but compare the look of it to the Cheshire cat in Alice in Wonderland. "You're going to do great, sweetie."

Neal clears his throat to get my attention. "You go home and rest, sweetheart. I will take care of everything. You said you are going to your father's house while you do your treatment?"

I nod and bite my lip. "Just as soon as I tell him."

# About The Author

Geri Glenn is the best-selling author of Kings Of Korruption MC Series.

Geri lives in beautiful New Brunswick, Canada. She is a military wife, the mother of two gorgeous, but slightly crazy little girls, and has been fortunate enough to finally quit her day job to stay home and do what she loves most - write!

Stalk her!

♛ Website: http://geriglenn.com

♛ Facebook: https://www.facebook.com/geriglennauthor

♛ Twitter: https://twitter.com/authorgeriglenn

♛ Instagram: https://instagram.com/authorgeriglenn/

♛ Amazon: amazon.com/author/geriglenn

♛ Mailing List: http://eepurl.com/bq5xgT

Keep Reading for an
Excerpt From:


Dani's Return
By Ariel Marie

# Chapter One

## Dani

She would never tire of the aroma of the early morning fresh air, or the blooming spring flowers.

*Mother nature at her best.*

Daniella Harper smiled as best she could in her wolf form. She trotted back towards the fence that separated her backyard from the open land of the Tennessee State National Forest.

She reached the stairs of her back porch before slowly morphing back into her human form. The warm rays of the sun felt amazing against her naked skin. She was lucky that she didn't have to worry about anyone seeing her in all her glory; her neighbors on each side of her home were about a half a mile down the road each way.

*And that was how she liked it.*

She walked into her back door, directly into her kitchen, and went over to the fridge to pull out a chilled bottle of water. A good long run always left her parched.

She grabbed her smartphone and hit the app that controlled her music, blasting it through the surround sound speakers throughout her home. She danced her way to her room and grabbed a towel so she could jump into the shower.

Twenty minutes later, she reappeared from her shower feeling refreshed. She threw on jeans and an oversized T-shirt that she tied in a knot at the base of her back. Another one of her favorite songs began to play as she grabbed her laptop and cell phone, and danced her way into the living room.

"Hello…it's me," she sang along, plopping down onto her couch. She booted up her computer when the old ringtone ringer of her phone cut the song short, signifying an incoming call.

"Aw, come on," she whined out loud, laughing at herself. But once she saw who was calling, her smile grew even wider. "What's up, BFF?" she answered.

"Hey, Dani," a familiar voice greeted her.

Hope Foster had been her best friend since they were six years old. They met at the beginning of first grade, and were inseparable while growing up. Hope and her family were human, and never treated Daniella, a shifter, any different.

Humans were well aware of the existence of shifters, and both species tried to live in peace with one another. Shifters preferred to live near the outskirts of towns and cities, or even out in the country to be near the open land in order to have safe places to run in their animal forms.

Of course, there were those anti-shifter groups that protested and rallied against shifters on the platform that shifters were a danger to the public, and should be made to register and live on reservations, away from humans. The pro-shifter groups argued that like humans, there were good and bad shifters. These groups felt that shifters should have the same treatment and rights as humans.

The Fosters' had always accepted Daniella, as if she were their second child. Growing up, she probably spent more time in their home than she did her own.

"How the hell are you, Hope?" she asked, logging into her job's website to fill out a few reports for work. She was a social worker for the local county children and family services in the shifter division. She needed to finish filling out her reports from her home visits that she did yesterday.

Hope's deep sigh reached Dani's ears and grabbed her wolf's attention. Something wasn't right. "Dani, it's Mom."

"What?" she almost screeched. Her heart pounded hard in her chest as she thought of the wonderful woman who was like a second mother to her. "Is she okay?"

Thoughts raced through her mind at the possibility that something was wrong with Mrs. Foster. She didn't think she would be able to handle it.

"She found a lump in her left breast a couple of weeks ago," Hope said, her voice sounding strained.

Her usual high-pitched, jolly voice was now dull, and almost lifeless. Dani's wolf whined, scratching at her from the inside, sensing that their best friend was in pain.

"Oh my God," she breathed into the phone. She squeezed her eyes shut. This could not be happening. "What is going on?"

"They did a mammogram, and it came back abnormal. There was a dense mass, and they suggested an ultrasound guided biopsy."

"Why didn't anyone call me sooner?" Dani whispered into the phone. Her vision blurred from tears that threatened to fall, and worry filled her chest, as she had already lost her parents tragically in a car accident. She couldn't lose Mrs. Foster too. She sat her laptop down on the coffee table and perched on the edge of the couch to listen.

"She didn't want anyone to know," Hope said, a small sniffle escaping. "She said she thought it would turn out to be nothing, and she didn't want to worry anyone. But it's been downhill since the mammogram."

"Did she have the biopsy yet? What did it say?"

"Yes, she had it," Hope paused again. Dani could hear her blow her nose before she came back to the phone. "It's cancer, and the mass is big enough that they want to try some chemo, or some type of drugs first before considering surgery. It has been a blur to me ever since we sat in the doctor's office when he explained everything."

"I'm coming home," Dani said without hesitation. She had been gone for too long from their small town of Wakefield, Ohio.

"You said you could never come back—"

"It doesn't matter. You are my family, and I must come home. I have to see her," she whispered into the phone. It was true. After her parents' died her senior year of high school, it was the Foster family who took her in so that she could finish out her last year of high school.

When she was twelve years old, her parents entered into an agreement with the alpha for her to mate with his son. She never got it out of them why the alpha wanted her for his son. They only insisted that it was an honor for her to be chosen for the future alpha of their pack, and with her as the alpha's mate, she could help turn their pack around. This had been the only thing that her and her parents had ever disagreed about. She begged and pleaded for them to break the arrangement, but they refused, stating that the arrangement was already made. There was nothing they could do to change it.

After graduating from high school, she packed her things and left Wakefield. She ran away, scared of what her future held as the mate of the future alpha. She didn't care about the agreement that that the alpha and her parents had. Her parents had died, and she refused to uphold that agreement.

Evan Torres, the alpha that made the mating arrangement with her parents, was a cruel, heartless man that was known in the Midwest as Crazy Torres. Junior, the alpha's son, was quickly following in his father's footsteps, and Dani refused to be mated to such an evil wolf.

Her life would have been a living hell if she had mated with Junior. He tormented her as a child, and she refused to spend her entire life with him. The Torres family had been in charge of the Blood Moon pack for generations, and drove the pack into the ground.

The Blood Moons were once a thriving pack, and had once held a reputation of being one of the strongest packs in the Midwest, but under the reign of the Torres family, the Blood Moons barely garnered respect.

Once she ran, she had always had to look over her shoulder for fear that Junior would show up and drag her back to Wakefield, which would have been his right in the eyes of shifter law. They had been promised to each other since she was twelve, and he was fourteen years old. The human laws upheld most of the Lycan laws, so whenever Junior decided to come for her, the human police would have no jurisdiction.

She knew that Junior had his wolves had been watching her. She always had a creepy sensation that someone's eyes were on her. Her wolf was always on the defense, never knowing if someone would jump out of the shadows to grab her and drag her back to Junior. She was always moving, trying to get away from Junior and his wolves, but no matter where she went, they would somehow find her.

About a year ago, she no longer had the sensation that someone was watching her, and the fear of being discovered vanished. One morning she woke up and just felt... *free*. She didn't know what was different, but she had taken advantage of it. She had even gone out and bought her dream house, and had finally begun to live life.

"Don't worry about me," she said, her voice growing stronger. "I'll be just fine."

Want more of Ariel Marie?

Visit her on Amazon!

www.amazon.com/author/arielmarie


or


Visit her website:

www.thearielmarie.com

# about the author

Avelyn Paige is a born and raised Indiana girl. While she may be a Hoosier by birth, she is a Boilermaker by choice. Boiler Up! She resides in a sleepy little town in Indiana with her husband and three crazy pets. Avelyn spends her days working as a cancer research scientist and her nights sipping moonshine while writing and book reviewing. Avelyn loves everything paranormal, Cajun culture, and wants to try tornado chasing as a hobby when she finally grows up. She just has to get over that pesky fear of thunderstorms first. Avelyn also enjoys collecting voodoo dolls from her trips to New Orleans.

Made in United States
Troutdale, OR
07/18/2023

11391780R00066